'S PRICE

NORMAN
PRICE

BELLA
LASAGNE

JAMES

SARAH

MEET ALL THESE FRIENDS IN BUZZ BOOKS:

Thomas the Tank Engine
The Animals of Farthing Wood
Biker Mice from Mars
Winnie-the-Pooh
Fireman Sam
Rupert
Babar

First published in Great Britain 1993 by Buzz Books
an imprint of Reed Children's Books
Michelin House, 81 Fulham Road, London SW3 6RB
and Auckland, Melbourne, Singapore and Toronto
Reprinted 1995

Fireman Sam copyright © 1985 Prism Art & Design Limited
Text and illustrations copyright © 1993 Reed International Books Limited
Based on the animation series produced by Bumper Films for
S4C/Channel 4 Wales and Prism Art & Design Limited
Original idea by Dave Gingell and Dave Jones, assisted by Mike Young
Characters created by Rob Lee
All rights reserved

ISBN 1 85591 321 6

Printed and bound in Italy by Olivotto

RIVER RESCUE

Story by Rob Lee
Illustrations by The County Studio

It was a sunny day in Pontypandy. On his way to the fire station, Fireman Sam popped into Mrs Price's shop to buy a morning newspaper.

"Morning, Dilys," said Fireman Sam. "It's a lovely day today."

"Is it?" Dilys replied. "I've been working so hard, I hadn't even noticed."

6

As Fireman Sam stepped outside the shop, Sarah and James came racing down the High Street on their bicycles.

"Look out, Uncle Sam," shouted James.

"Great fires of London!" Fireman Sam exclaimed. Quickly, he leapt out of the way, accidentally knocking into a crate of Dilys Price's best tomatoes!

"Sorry, Uncle Sam," apologised Sarah.

"Me too," said James.

"Why don't you two go for a ride in the countryside?" Sam suggested. "You're less likely to run into someone there."

"Good idea, Uncle Sam," said James. "Come on, Sarah."

The twins turned round and rode out of the village.

CARROTS

Later that morning, Sam walked into the mess hall at the fire station.

"Breakfast smells delicious," he remarked.

"That's because Elvis didn't cook it," said Station Officer Steele. He handed Sam a dish. "He's gone to Newtown to collect a consignment of spare tyres."

"I hope he's not going to use the tyres in a new recipe," laughed Sam, as he tucked into his breakfast.

9

Firefighter Elvis Cridlington had picked up
the tyres from Newtown and was now on
his way back to Pontypandy. He steered
Jupiter up the bumpy road beside Pandy
River. When he spotted Sarah and James
coming towards him on their bicycles, he
stopped to say hello.

10

"Hi, Sarah! Hi, James!" he called.

"Hi, Elvis," shouted Sarah. "We're having a race and I'm winning."

"No, she's not!" called James.

"Yes, I am!" replied Sarah.

Elvis chuckled and waved, then continued on his way.

11

"Pontypandy here I come," whistled Elvis. "I'll bet Fireman Sam and Station Officer Steele missed not having my special cooked breakfast this morning," he thought, as the big red fire engine bumped along the road.

At the top of the hill, Jupiter bounced over an especially big bump, causing the locker door to fly open. Elvis didn't notice as the tyres tumbled out of the locker and rolled back down the hill towards the river.

Sarah and James were racing along at full
speed when they spotted some tyres rolling
down the hill past them. From the corner
of his eye, James could see that there were
more tyres coming down the hill behind
them, and they were gaining speed! The
twins had to do something — and quickly!

"Watch out!" cried James.

The twins swerved out of the way.

"Oh no!" cried Sarah as her bike crashed into a hedge.

"Whooah!" yelled James.

He careered out of control down the embankment. James and his bike landed in the river with a mighty SPLASH!

The current carried James downriver.
Finally, he managed to grab onto a tree
branch that was overhanging the water.
But the branch was slippery and James had
to fight against the current. He didn't know
how long he'd be able to hold on!

"Help!" he cried. "Sarah, get help!"

Sarah climbed out of the hedge and raced
to the river. "Hang on, James!" she called.
"I'll go and ring the fire brigade!"

At the fire station, Fireman Sam had come out to the forecourt to help Elvis unload the tyres.

"It looks like you forgot the tyres, Elvis," said Sam, pointing to the empty locker.

"That's funny," replied Elvis. "I'm sure they were there when I left Newtown."

18

Just then Station Officer Steele sounded the alarm.

"Jump to it!" he cried. "James has fallen into Pandy River!"

"Great fires of London!" cried Sam as he and Elvis jumped aboard Jupiter. They sped out of the station, sirens wailing.

As Jupiter raced towards the river, Elvis
spotted the tyres scattered beside the road.
"Look, we've found my tyres!" he said.

Sam parked Jupiter near the bridge where Sarah was waiting.

"Hurry, Uncle Sam!" she cried.

"Don't worry, Sarah," replied Sam. "We'll soon have James on dry land."

Quickly, the firefighters unloaded the ladders from Jupiter. But even the longest extension ladder didn't reach James.

"Daro!" groaned Elvis. "What are we going to do now?"

"Help!" James cried. "I can't hang on much longer."

Suddenly, Fireman Sam had an idea.

Sam sprang into action. He grabbed one of
the tyres from the roadside and tied a long
rope around it. Then he threw the tyre
into the water from upriver. He held on
tightly to the end of the rope as the
current swept the tyre towards James.

Still holding onto the tree branch with
one hand, James reached out for the tyre
with the other.

22

"It's working!" said Elvis, as the current carried the tyre to James.

"Put the tyre over your head, James, and hold on tight!" shouted Sam.

Fireman Sam, Elvis and Station Officer
Steele lined up in a row on the riverbank.
They pulled the rope as hard and as fast as
they could until they had towed James
safely onto the bank.

"Quick thinking, Sam," said Steele as they
lifted James out of the water.

"Thanks, Uncle Sam," said James. "You
saved me!"

"Luckily there's no harm done," said Sam,
as he wrapped a blanket around a very wet
James. "Are you all right, Sarah?"

"I'm okay, but my bike's not," she replied.
"It's got a bent front wheel."

"And mine's got a bent back wheel,"
groaned James, as he examined his bike.

"It's all my fault," moaned Elvis. "I should have made sure that the tyres were safely locked in the locker."

Sam rubbed his chin thoughtfully. "Let's go home and I'll see what I can do with the bikes," he said.

Sam and Elvis loaded them into Jupiter and they all drove back to Pontypandy.

26

The next day at the fire station, Elvis made the twins an ice cream sundae treat for the trouble he'd caused them.

"My favourite!" said Sarah.

"Mine too!" said James.

"And when you've finished, we've got a special surprise for you," said Elvis, with a mysterious grin.

When the twins had finished their sundaes,
they followed Elvis to the station forecourt.

"Where's our special surprise?" asked
James excitedly.

"Well, I'm afraid we couldn't straighten
the wheels on your bikes," Elvis told the
twins. "But Sam did the next best thing."

Fireman Sam and Station Officer Steele
appeared riding a strange-looking bicycle.

"I couldn't fix your bikes," said Sam, "so I
made a tandem!"

"Brill!" said James.

"Fantastic!" exclaimed Sarah. "It'll be the
only one in Pontypandy!"

FIREMAN SAM

STATION OFFICER
STEELE

TREVOR EVANS

ELVIS
CRIDLINGTON

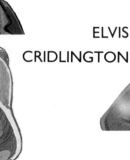

PENNY MORRIS